The Bogeyman

Written by Mij Kelly

Illustrated by Keino

In the middle of a game in the back lane,
Carrie said to Harry, "Don't step on the lines."
And the world changed.

"Don't step on the lines," said Carrie,
"or the Bogeyman will get you."
"Who's the Bogeyman?" asked Harry.

"The Bogeyman," said Carrie, "is as thin as a knife. He waits all his life in the cracks between things. He has eyes like fried eggs and hair like string. He waits and he takes his time until the day that you tread on a line. Then – SNIP SNAP! – just like that, up he jumps and gets you."

"OK," said Harry. "That's fine. I'll take care not to step on a line."

Afterwards, when he walked down the street,
he took great care where he put his feet.
He hip-hopped to the shops.
He tiptoed at the swimming pool.

And on the days when he went to school, he always took a flying leap – and landed safely in his seat.

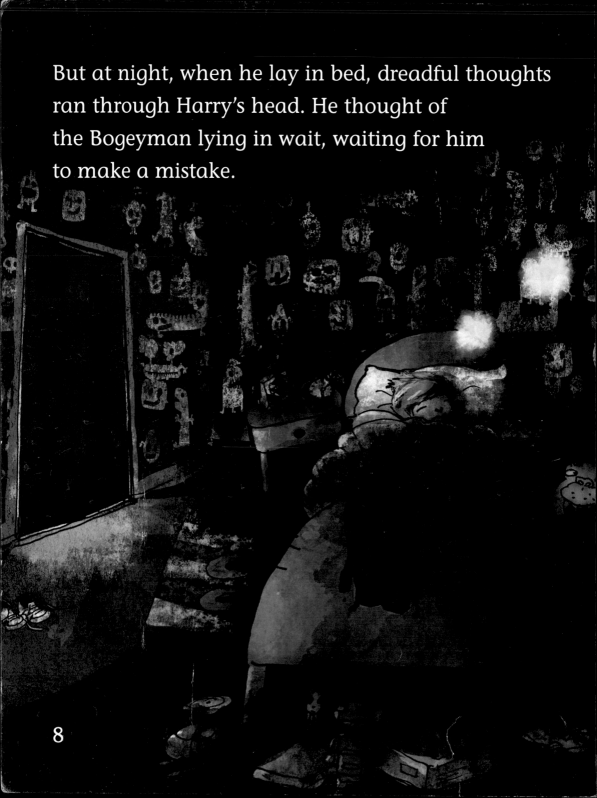

But at night, when he lay in bed, dreadful thoughts ran through Harry's head. He thought of the Bogeyman lying in wait, waiting for him to make a mistake.

Every line was a trap, every crack was a threat,
and when Harry slept …
   in his dreams
      he watched
         his step.

And little by little, Harry's fright oozed out of the night and into the day, rising up through the cracks when he was trying to play.

When he told Carrie, she laughed and said he
was daft. She said the Bogeyman was only a game.
And Harry felt embarrassed. He felt ashamed.

So he acted brave. He huffed and puffed.
He pretended he was really tough.
"I'm not afraid of fried eggs. I'm not afraid of string.
I'm not afraid of ANYTHING!"

13

SNIP SNAP! Just like that, Harry fell into
the Bogeyman's trap.
He landed on his feet …

on a crack

and all his fear came rushing back.

15

Harry ran. He didn't wait for the Bogeyman.
He didn't watch his feet; he didn't watch his step.
He flew down the street. He trod on cracks.
He trod on gaps.

He trod on every single line.
He didn't have time –
the Bogeyman was chasing behind!

SNIP SNAP!

Harry ran like the wind and hurled himself into
the safest place in the world.
He curled up small and waited.
He covered his eyes … but nothing happened.
The clock tick-tocked, his mother sighed and Harry
realised he was still alive.

His fear slipped away through the cracks and into the floor. And the world changed back to how it was before.

Now, whenever Carrie says, "I expect there's a monster under your bed." Or, "There's a man behind you made out of worms."

Harry doesn't even turn. He doesn't even blink.
He stops and he thinks. He laughs and he laughs.
He says, "Come on, Carrie. I'm not that daft!"

Harry and the Bogeyman

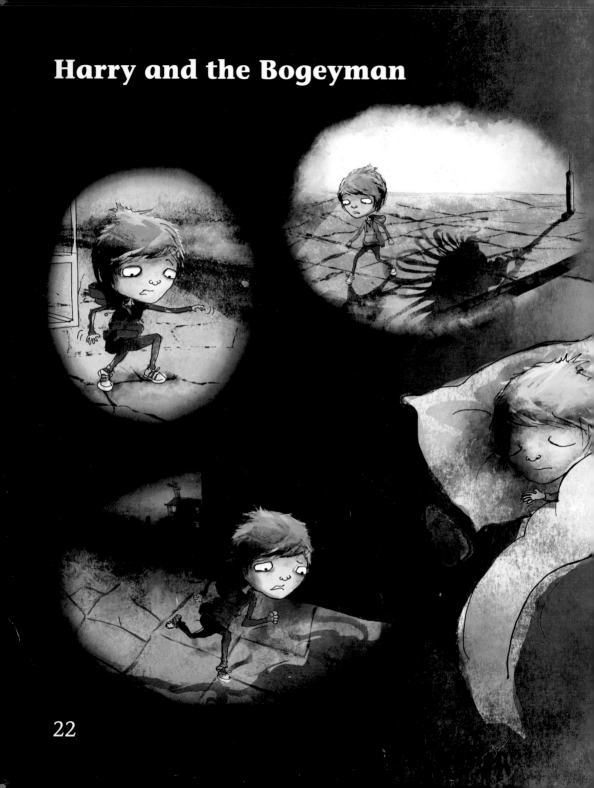

Ideas for reading

Written by Clare Dowdall BA(Ed), MA(Ed)
Lecturer and Primary Literacy Consultant

Learning objectives: read independently and with increasing fluency longer and less familiar texts; know how to tackle unfamiliar words that are not completely decodable; draw together ideas and information from across a whole text; give some reasons why things happen or characters change; tell real and imagined stories using the conventions of familiar story language

Curriculum links: Citizenship: Choices

Interest words: Bogeyman, snip snap, hip-hopped, dreadful, oozed, embarrassed, ashamed, tick-tocked

Word count: 477

Resources: ICT

Getting started

- Tell children a brief story from your own childhood about something that frightened you that wasn't a real threat, e.g. a noisy night-time radiator. Sensitively, ask children if they have memories of being scared about anything that wasn't real.

- Look at the front cover together. Discuss the shadow in the illustration. What could it be, and how do they think Harry feels about it? Ask children what they think a Bogeyman is and to describe what they think the Bogeyman in the story looks and behaves like.

- Using the blurb, model how to read the speech with expression and emphasise the internal rhyme for effect. Explain that there are lots of hidden rhyming words in this story and that they create a dramatic effect when read with emphasis.

- Look at the word *Bogeyman* together. Remind children of some strategies for tackling longer unfamiliar words, e.g. using phonic strategies, looking for units of meaning, breaking the word into syllables before blending, using contextual cues.

Reading and responding

- Read pp2–3 together. Help children to understand what is happening and in particular the sentence, "And the world changed." Discuss how Harry's world changed, and clarify that he is suddenly aware of the Bogeyman.